Stranger in the Glen

by
Kirsty White

Illustrations by Martin Remphry

W
FRANKLIN WATTS
LONDON • NEW YORK • SYDNEY

Stranger in the Glen

First published in 1997 by Franklin Watts

This paperback edition published in 1998

Franklin Watts
96 Leonard Street
London EC2A 4RH

Franklin Watts Australia
14 Mars Road
Lane Cove
NSW 2006

Editor: Kyla Barber
Series editor: Paula Borton
Designer: Kirstie Billingham
Consultant: Douglas Ansdell

A CIP catalogue record for this book
is available from the British Library.

ISBN   0 7496 3123 6 (pbk)
       0 7496 2586 4 (hbk)

Dewey Classification 941.106

Printed in Great Britain

1

An Unwelcome Visitor

There was a stranger in the glen. Catriona watched as her father went to talk to the man wearing the plaid of red and black tartan. She wasn't close enough to hear what was said, but after a time her father shrugged and threw his arms up in a gesture

of despair and the stranger strode away.
Catriona fell in beside her father as he
walked back to their house.

"What's the matter?" she asked him.

"Ach, dearest, it's nothing for you to
worry about," he said, smiling brightly
although his expression had been grim.
"You go and fetch Rory while I talk to your
mother. It's nearly dinner time."

After her father had gone inside the house, Catriona put two fingers to her lips and whistled to Rory to tell him to come home. Then she crept towards the window to listen.

"That was Rob Roy's man," her father said.

Catriona gasped. She'd often heard talk of the outlaw and his band of men, but she had never seen any of them before.

"He wants a hundred merks' blackmail this year," her father was saying.

"The cheek of it!" Catriona's mother said. "That's robbery, so it is."

"Aye, but what choice do I have? If I don't pay him, the cattle won't make it to market. They'll disappear on the way."

Catriona heard the sound of footsteps. She turned and saw her younger brother running towards her. "Ssshh," she hissed.

"What's going on?" asked Rory.

She glared at him, shaking her head vigorously.

"What is it?" Rory insisted.

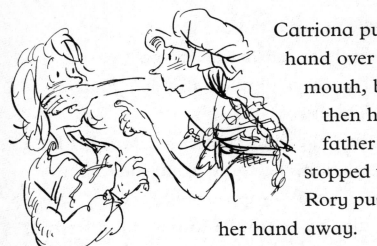

Catriona put her hand over his mouth, but by then her father had stopped talking. Rory pushed her hand away.

"What's happening?"

"I'm not sure," she said. "I didn't catch all of it, you made such a racket."

"What *did* you catch?" Rory demanded.

"That man," she told him, "he's one of Rob Roy's men. They want a hundred merks to let the cattle through the pass."

"So?"

Catriona sighed. "We can't afford it. But if we don't pay, they'll steal the cattle."

"Can't the cattle go another way?"

"Don't be daft," Catriona said.

"There is no other way."

Tam, the cattle drover, came to the house after dinner, when Catriona was supposed to be asleep in the big bed at the end of the house. Rory slept on a mattress at the far end of the bed. She looked over and saw that he was awake too.

Tam's voice drifted towards them. "It's just too risky," he said. "If you don't pay, that rascal will have the lot of them."

"I offered him fifty," her father said. "He said he'd talk to Rob about it and let me know."

"Aye, but when? The market's over in a couple of days. If you miss the market, the buyers'll be gone."

"Ach," her father said, "I thought with the warrant out for his arrest, the man would have tamed down a bit."

"It would take more than an arrest warrant to tame yon," Tam said grimly.

The two men talked some more, then Tam got up to leave, calling for his dog, Queenie, who sat waiting by the door. Catriona was thinking hard.

"What's an arrest warrant?" Rory whispered.

"Rob Roy stole some money, so there's soldiers out looking for him."

"Why isn't he hiding, then?"

"You know how many friends he's got. He'd be long gone before they got anywhere near him."

Rory laughed.

"It's not funny," Catriona said. "If we pay the blackmail, we can't pay the rent, and if we don't pay, then we lose the cattle, so we can't pay the rent anyway."

"Unless we sneak past Rob Roy," Rory said.

2

Mission by Moonlight

At last the house was silent. Everyone was
asleep and the moon was high in the sky.
Catriona shook Rory awake.

"What is it?" he mumbled.

"Ssshh," she whispered. "We're going
to take the cattle to market ourselves."

"But Rob Roy will be on the look-out."

"Yes, but he'll be looking for Tam, not us. He won't be watching the hill path. Come on, it was your idea."

Rory rubbed the sleep from his eyes, then he grinned.

"Hurry up," Catriona said. "We have to be back by dawn, else they'll begin to get worried."

Catriona and Rory slipped on their clothes and crept out of the house without disturbing their mother and father. Catriona was nervous. Even Rob Roy had to sleep, she told herself, and her father would be so pleased when she told him that the cattle were safely to market without a penny blackmail being paid.

Rory began to whistle. She told him to hush until they were well away from the houses. If anyone woke up and saw them, that would be the end of it.

The cattle were sleeping in the meadow. Their shaggy coats were wet with the evening dew.

"Do we take them all?" Rory asked her.

"No, stupid, just the stirks," Catriona said. She'd brought a stick with her, and she began prodding the calves to one side and the cows to the other. She had often watched Tam do the same, but it wasn't as easy as it looked. The calves resented her commands, and the cows began to low in protest.

When she turned her back for a moment, the calves wandered back to their mothers. Rory started to giggle.

"Tam uses Queenie to keep them together," He said helpfully.

Catriona frowned. She'd forgotten that the old drover always worked with his dog.

"I could go and get her," he said.

"All right," Catriona said crossly, "but hurry."

When Rory came back with the dog, Catriona was standing between the cows and the calves, waving her stick threateningly. Queenie seemed to know just what to do. She wagged her tail and then nipped at the hocks of the nearest calves, w began to move slowly away. The cows, sad that they were losing their young, began to low in earnest.

The racket they made echoed through the glen. Catriona could do nothing to stop it – she just had to pray that the grown-ups wouldn't wake up.

By the time they reached the hill path above the forest, the sound of the cows had faded. Queenie ran around the calves to keep them together, so fast that she was almost a blur. The path was narrow so they moved in a long line with Catriona at its head, Rory bringing up the rear and the dog running between them. The moon lit their way. In the forest, wild animals paused in their foraging, amazed at the invasion.

By the time the moon had set, they were half-way to the town. Suddenly there was a movement in the grass and Queenie flashed after it. Catriona waited, but the dog did not come back and the calves came to a halt in a confused knot.

"What happened?" she asked Rory.

"A hare," he said. "You know what Queenie's like."

"Go and find her," Catriona ordered. Without the dog, the calves were already beginning to stray.

Rory ran off into the forest, whistling and calling. Catriona began to run back and forth along the line of calves, as Queenie had done, waving her stick and yelling to try to

keep them together. She was not as fast as
the dog, and when she got to the end, the
calves at the front would scatter. Then,
when she went to gather them together,
the calves at the back turned on their heels
and began to make their way back towards
their mothers. Catriona ran to and fro
frantically. In a short time she was
completely out of breath.

Rory came back without Queenie.

"She's gone," he said.

Catriona had
a sudden vision
of what old
Tam would
do when he
found out that
she had lost
his precious dog.

"Rory, we have to
find her," she gasped.

"She'll be miles
away by now," he said matter-of-factly.

Catriona groaned.

"Tam says that when she starts
chasing hares, she won't come home
until she's exhausted." Rory went on.
"That's why he never brings her anywhere
near here."

"Now you tell me."

"I forgot," Rory said.

It was too late to go back. Without Queenie, they wouldn't make it home by morning, nor would they get to market.

Rory read Catriona's thoughts. "What do we do now?" he asked.

3

A Walk in the Forest

The forest was their only hope. It stretched all the way down to the shores of Loch Lomond and in amongst the trees nobody would see them.

"We'll hide," Catriona said.

Rory frowned.

"Come on," she said. "I'll lead the
way. You go at the back. Mind you
don't let them stray."

Catriona ran back and forth trying to
keep the cattle together. She thought she
had better count them, so that she'd know if
any went missing. After several attempts she
decided there were forty-eight.

The trees were thick with new growth

and Catriona had to push the branches aside to make way for the calves. They followed her reluctantly, after a great deal of pulling and prodding.

A few yards into the forest, the ground fell away sharply and the grass was slippery with dew. Catriona had to grab at a branch to keep herself upright and

the calves slithered and slid into each other, mooing in surprise.

Under the trees, it was very dark and the air was chill. Catriona shivered and stumbled on, pausing every so often to count the cattle. Only when they came to a clearing did she realise that morning had come. Far above, the sky was silver with the sunrise.

"We'll stop here," she said.

Catriona counted the cattle. There were only forty-seven. She counted again, and then told Rory that he had lost one.

"I'll go and find it," he said, yawning.

"No," she said. "I will. You watch the rest of them."

She climbed all the way back to the path, but there was no sign of the missing calf. When she got back to the clearing, Rory was fast asleep and the rest of the cattle were gone.

"Oh, no," she moaned as she shook him awake. Rory blinked and looked around.

"Quickly," she said. "We have to find them."

There wasn't time to be angry. The cattle had left tracks in the dewy grass. They followed, finding them a little way down the hill, heading for the loch.

"They must be thirsty," Rory said.

"They'll just have to wait," Catriona said.

Rob Roy guarded the loch road. If he caught them there he'd not only demand blackmail but confiscate some of the cattle as well, because they'd tried to slip past him. She grabbed the nearest calf and tried to point its head down to show it that there was plenty of moisture on the damp grass. The calf struggled. Rather than

waste more time Catriona began to drive
them all back to the clearing. It took a long
time to get there because the cattle were
intent on going in the other direction. When
she counted them, there were only forty-six.

"Taigh na galla!" Catriona muttered.

Rory looked at her. "What did you say?"

"Nothing."

She counted the cattle again. Still forty-six. For a moment, she wondered whether to look for the missing calves, then decided that if she did she'd risk losing more. The market was only a couple of miles away. Once night came, they'd be there in no time at all.

Catriona and Rory sat down at the edge of the clearing, with the cattle herded before them.

"We mustn't sleep," Catriona said.

"Of course not," Rory agreed.

As the sun rose, the day became warm
and balmy. The cattle seemed to settle at
last, lying down to bask in the sunshine.

As the calves fell asleep, so did
Catriona and Rory.

4

The Calves Have Ideas of Their Own

Catriona woke first. She wondered why
she felt so stiff and what had happened
to her blanket. Then she opened her eyes
and saw the sky and remembered where
she was.

It was midday or afterwards, the sun

was already heading westwards and the
cattle were nowhere to be seen apart from
just one who slept contentedly on the grass.

Catriona woke Rory and then they
raced down to the
loch. The dew
had dried and
they could no
longer see the tracks
of the calves.
They just had
to hope they'd
gone that way.

Their father's cattle were drinking happily from the loch on the other side of the road.

"Go and bring them back," Catriona hissed at Rory.

"What if Rob Roy's watching?"

"He's not or he'd be away with them."

"You go," Rory said.

Catriona bit back an angry retort. "You go," she told him. "You're just a boy. He wouldn't hurt you."

"You're just a girl," Rory said. "He wouldn't hurt you either."

Catriona glared at her brother, but he just stood there. Finally she shook her head and then, very slowly, stepped out into the road. When she was sure that no one was watching, she crossed over and gathered the cattle together and began to drive them back to the forest. Rory watched her.

"Don't just stand there," she snapped. "Help me."

He moved off and began to wave his staff at the calves.

When they got back to the clearing, the calf that had been sleeping had vanished. Catriona cursed again.

"By the time we get to the market in Drymen there won't be any left," Rory said.

"Shut up!" she snarled, glowering at the calves as if to dare them to move so

much as a muscle.

"I'm hungry," Rory said.

Catriona's fists clenched in anger.

Her stomach was grumbling too, and she envied the cattle who ate only grass. She paced around the herd, trying to keep her mind off the thought of food.

At last the sun moved beyond the edge of the clearing.

"It won't be much longer," she said to Rory. "When we get to Drymen we'll buy some scones."

Rory's face lit up. She smiled at him, thinking that if they hurried they might reach the town before everyone had gone to bed.

There was a soft rustle in the grass, as if a deer was coming. Catriona stopped her pacing and listened. The sound ceased. She began to walk once more and then she heard it again, louder this time, too loud for a deer that would in any case have fled at the sight of humans. She stopped and held her finger to her lips.

There was silence for a moment and then Catriona heard another rustle, just behind her. She swung round and saw a red-haired man wearing a plaid of red and black tartan. His face was like thunder.

Rob Roy!

The sound of panicked footsteps told Catriona that Rory had fled.

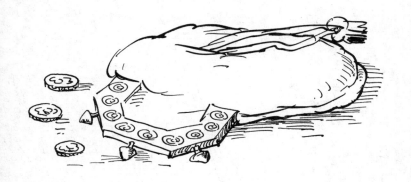

5

Caught!

Rob Roy stood glaring at her, surrounded by his men.

"Who are you?" he asked, in a voice that was laden with anger.

"Catriona Lamond," she murmured.

"Lamond of Rowardennan?"

Catriona nodded.

"Yon who said he couldn't afford my fees?"

Catriona said nothing.

"I know he's mean but I never dreamed he'd try a cowardly trick like this!"

Beyond her fear, Catriona felt anger. "My father's not mean," she said, "and he's not a coward either."

"Oh, no? Who else would send his cattle with nought but a young girl and a lad to guard them?"

Catriona was speechless. Rob Roy stood there, bold as brass, counting her cattle. "Forty-five prime stirks," he said. "They'll fetch a good price, together with the five we found wandering."

That's two more than I lost, Catriona thought, but she didn't tell him that.

Rob Roy shook his head. "If your

father had paid me he'd have the money by now. This way, he'll not see a penny of it." He told one of his men to herd the cattle together, then he turned back to her.

"Away with you, lass, before I decide to charge your father a ransom."

Trembling inside, Catriona thought of what her father would say when she got home and told him that she'd lost his cattle. She'd been so sure that she would save him from having to pay blackmail. Now they wouldn't be able to pay the rent, never mind buy salt and meal for the winter.

She began to take a step and then she stopped.

"Get out of my sight," Rob Roy said, "afore I change my mind."

Catriona stood up as straight as she could and met his gaze with one of her own.

"No," she said.

"What?"

"I said, no."

"What d'you mean, no?"

"I mean," Catriona said slowly, "I'm not going to go. If you take the cattle, I'll follow you to Drymen and I'll tell whoever buys them that you stole them."

"Now, wait a minute," Rob Roy said. "I offered your father a fair deal and he didn't want it, so I've a right to his cattle."

"You have not," Catriona said. "It wasn't a fair deal, it was robbery! A hundred merks, and you know we'd not get much more than that for the cattle. How are we supposed to pay the rent? How are we supposed to eat this winter?"

One of Rob Roy's men moved to silence Catriona, but Rob Roy shook his head.

"I need the money," he said.

"You do not! You stole a thousand pounds from Montrose only last year."

Rob Roy's eyes narrowed into angry slits but Catriona did not flinch.

Rob Roy sighed. "Now," he said, "tell me the truth. Does your father know you're away with his cattle?"

Catriona looked away. "No," she said.

"What are you doing with them, then?"

Catriona took a deep breath and told him that her father just couldn't afford to pay the blackmail, that he could only afford half of it, and even then it would be a struggle. She decided to take the cattle herself, because Rob Roy wouldn't be expecting a girl and he wouldn't be

watching the hill path anyway. She
finished by saying that Rob Roy had a
heck of a cheek charging anything because
he didn't even own the land. Like her
mother said, blackmail
was robbery.

Rob Roy looked at her for a long
time, then he smiled. "We've been
watching you all night," he said. "At first
we thought Lamond was up to something,

but when we saw it was just you two, we wondered what was going on. Nobody in his right mind would send a herd of cattle off with two bairns in charge of them."

Catriona smiled too, but she was a bit annoyed about being called a baby.

Rob Roy folded his arms. "I'll give you a deal. Give me half the cattle and I'll let you through to Drymen."

"That's more than fifty merks," Catriona said slowly.

"The price is a hundred," Rob Roy said.

Catriona said nothing.

"All right," he said, "just because it's you, we'll shake hands on fifteen."

Catriona shook her head.

"Why not? That's a fair bargain!"

"They're not my cattle to give you!"

"My, but you're a hard woman," he said. "I'll settle for ten."

Catriona faced him bravely. "I don't see why I should give you any. We didn't go along your road and we're nearly at Drymen."

Rob Roy's eyes narrowed. "But you're not there yet. If I don't take you, you might meet up with bandits."

"The only bandit around here is you!"

For a moment he looked darkly at her and then he grinned. "Don't tell anyone I let you through without paying me a penny," he said.

Catriona smiled in triumph. Rob Roy told two of his men to take her to Drymen, where she sold the cattle for more than a hundred merks.

Rob Roy waited for them just outside the town and then he walked Catriona back to Rowardennan.

On the way, she handed him two merks. "What's this?" he asked her.

"You gave us five cattle back, but we'd only lost three. That's the money for the other two."

He shook his head and then he cuffed her playfully.

When they neared her father's farm, Rob Roy said that he would leave her. Just before he did, he told her that it wasn't he who had stolen the £1,000 from Montrose, but a rogue who had once worked for him. Because Montrose thought that Rob Roy was a trustworthy fellow, he'd put the story around to try to force him to pay the money back. But times were hard and Rob Roy didn't have £1,000. He didn't even have

the 100 merks he'd tried to charge Catriona's father in blackmail.

"You've no idea," he said, "how hard life is if you're an outlaw."

Catriona smiled.

"If you ever want a job, let me know," he said. "I could always use a girl like you."

Catriona thanked him, then she walked slowly home, thinking that she would kill Rory when she saw him. But, first, she would have to explain everything to her father.

As Catriona approached the house, Queenie came rushing towards her, barking a welcome. But when her father came out he looked less pleased to see her.

"And where have you been?" he asked with a face like fury.

For a moment Catriona considered running away to join Rob Roy. Then she smiled brightly.

"I sold the cattle," she said. "I got a hundred merks for them. And I didn't pay a penny blackmail!"

Scotland in Rob Roy's Time

In 1707 England and Scotland were united and the two countries were governed by the Parliament and King in London. The Act of Union was only accepted by the Scottish Parliament as a result of bribery and

 threats – the majority of the Scottish people were against the idea. In 1708, the Jacobites (supporters of the exiled Stewart king) attempted a rising, but it collapsed in chaos. Other risings in 1715 and 1719 also failed. The country was poor; the average Scot was more concerned with survival than politics. Also, there was constant feuding within Scotland itself, not only between Lowlanders and Highlanders, but also amongst the Highland clans.

Life in the Highlands

Highland Chiefs lived in draughty, uncomfortable castles. The people lived in one-room buildings called black houses. Black houses had thick walls to withstand the bitter weather, and roofs thatched with heather. There was a single hearthless fire without a chimney, just a hole in the roof. In the winter the family cow usually shared the home.

In Rob Roy's time, the people lived on a diet of oatmeal, a little meat or fish, milk and some cheese. There was a whisky distillery in every village. There were also some parish and charity schools, but few children attended them.

Rob Roy MacGregor

Rob Roy MacGregor was born in 1671. By then the Clan MacGregor had been outlawed for hundreds of years, because they had a terrible reputation for being thieves and bandits. At first Rob Roy made a good living in the cattle trade, but his business collapsed in 1712 when the Duke of Montrose accused him of theft. After that, Rob Roy was constantly on the run from the law and Montrose's men. He made a living by charging a fee, 'blackmail', to permit cattle though areas that he controlled. In the story, Rob Roy demands a blackmail in merks – these were old Scottish coins.

Rob Roy was arrested only once, but later escaped. He died in 1734.

Gaelic

In the eighteenth century, the Gaelic language was spoken throughout the Highlands and also in parts of the Lowlands, such as Galloway and Ayrshire. But Gaelic went into decline because English was made the official language and children were taught English in school. Also, hundreds of thousands of Gaelic speakers were driven away from their land in the Highland Clearances of the nineteenth century.

However, Gaelic is still spoken in the Highlands and Islands of Scotland today.

Ciamar a tha thu?
How are you?

Tha gu math.
I am well.

('Taigh na galla' is a Gaelic oath or curse. Catriona uses it on page 34.)

The Highland Clans

Clans were groups of people who lived together under the rule of a Chief. The Chief's word was law, and he was judged on the strength of the fighting men that he could lead into battle.
The Highland clans were constantly feuding with each other. The biggest of these clans was Clan Donald, whose members bear the name McDonald or MacDonald. Mc or Mac means 'son of'.